What Are Literature Pockets?

In *Literature Pockets—Aesop's Fables,* eight fables come alive through fun, exciting projects. The activities for each fable are stored in a labeled pocket made from construction paper. (See directions below.) Add the charming cover and fasten the pockets together to make a personalized Aesop's Fables book for each student to enjoy.

How to Make the Pockets

1. Use a 12" x 18" (30.5 x 45.5 cm) piece of construction paper for each pocket. Fold up 6" (15 cm) to make a 12" (30.5 cm) square.
2. Staple the right side of the pocket closed.
3. Punch two or three holes in the left side of the pocket.

How to Make the Cover

1. Reproduce the cover illustration on page 3 for each student.
2. Have students color and cut out the illustration and glue it onto a 12" (30.5 cm) square piece of construction paper to make the cover.
3. Punch two or three holes in the left side of the cover.
4. Fasten the cover and the pockets together. You might use string, ribbon, twine, raffia, or metal rings.

How to Use Literature Pockets
Aesop's Fables

Step 1

Assemble a blank pocket book for each student. (See page 1.)

Step 2

Choose the first story you want to study. Reproduce the pocket label/bookmark page for students. Have students color and cut out the label and glue it onto the first pocket in their book.

Step 3

Complete the pocket.

- Have students color and cut out the bookmark and glue it onto a 4½" x 12" (11.5 x 30.5 cm) strip of construction paper. Have them use the bookmark to preview and review the story characters.

- Reproduce the story for students and read it together. Students may track the text with the edge of their bookmark.

- Have students do the follow-up activities and place the paperwork in the pocket with their bookmark and story.

Aesop's Fables

Name _____

The Tortoise and the Hare

Pocket Label and Bookmark .... **page 5**
Have students use these reproducibles to make
The Tortoise and the Hare pocket label and bookmark.
(See page 2.)

**The Story of
The Tortoise and the Hare** .... **pages 6–8**
Share and discuss this fable about an overconfident
hare and a persistent tortoise. Reproduce the story on
pages 7 and 8 for students. Use the teaching ideas on
page 6 to preview, read, and review the story. Follow
up with the "More to Explore" activities.

What Is the Moral? .... **pages 9 and 10**
Use this reproducible to review the meaning of the
fable's moral with students. Have students rewrite the
moral in their own words and then apply it to real-life
situations.

The Winner! .... **pages 11 and 12**
Students create a medal for the tortoise for winning the
race. Gather real medals for students to examine and
compare. (Check with students' parents.)

**Describe the Tortoise
and the Hare** .... **pages 13 and 14**
The tortoise and the hare looked and acted differently
from each other. Students explore these differences as
they complete a T-chart.

At the Races .... **page 15**
It's off to the races! Students discuss and compare
various kinds of races and then write about a real or
make-believe race.

The Tortoise and the Hare

Story characters:

Tortoise

Hare

Moral of the story:

Slow and steady wins the race.

I liked this story:

☐ Yes

☐ No

This bookmark belongs to

_____

(your name)

Share The Tortoise and the Hare

Preview the Story

State the title of the fable, and have students read aloud the names of the characters listed on the bookmark. Distribute copies of the fable (pages 7 and 8), and have students preview the pictures. Invite students who are unfamiliar with the fable to predict the outcome of the race between the tortoise and the hare.

Read the Story

Read the fable aloud as students follow along. Encourage students to track the text and underline or frame key words. List and discuss any unfamiliar words, such as *boasted*, *marked*, *steadily*, *wondered*, and *pokey*. Point out picture clues and context clues that help explain parts of the fable. After you have read the fable aloud, encourage students to reread it independently or with a partner.

Review the Story

Ask questions such as the following to help students recall important details about the characters, setting, and plot of the fable. Remind students that the *characters* are "who is in the story," the *setting* is "where the story takes place," and the *plot* is "what happens in a story."

- Who are the main characters of the fable?
- Where does the story take place?
- Why do you think Hare always bragged to the other animals?
- Why do you think Tortoise challenged Hare to a race?
- Who won the race? How?
- What do you think Hare was thinking before the race? After the race?
- What do you think Tortoise was thinking before the race? After the race?

More to Explore

- About Aesop

  Display the information at right about Aesop. Have students copy it onto paper and then draw a picture of Aesop to go with the description. Encourage students to go to the library or go online to research more about Aesop and his fables.

> ### Aesop
> Many of the fables we read today are thought to have first been told by a man named Aesop who lived as a slave in Greece over two thousand years ago. He was famous for the fables he told. The fables helped him win his freedom. Because fables have been handed down orally (told aloud) for centuries, you can find many versions of each tale throughout the world.

- Real or Make-Believe?

  Animals in fables do things real animals cannot, such as talk and run in races. Work with students to complete a large T-chart comparing fabled animals to real animals. Keep the chart and add on information as students read each fable.

The Tortoise and the Hare

The Tortoise and the Hare

One day, Hare was showing off to the other animals in the forest.

"I am the fastest animal in the forest," he boasted loudly. "No one can beat me in a race."

Slow-moving Tortoise was passing by. He heard what Hare said. "I know someone who can beat you in a race," he said quietly. "I can."

Hare fell down laughing at such an idea. "You think you can beat me? Very well," said Hare. "I'll race you, and I'll win!"

The next day, the other animals marked off a path for the race. Tortoise and Hare stood at the starting line. "Get ready. Get set. Go!" shouted Squirrel. Off raced Hare as fast as he could go. Soon he was so far ahead of slow-moving Tortoise that he could not see him.

"I think I'll take a little nap under this tree," thought Hare. "Tortoise is so far behind, he'll never catch up." Soon Hare was fast asleep.

Slowly but steadily Tortoise moved along the path. He saw Hare sleeping under the tree. Quietly he passed the sleeping Hare and went on his way. When Hare woke up from his nap, he couldn't see Tortoise anywhere.

"I knew that silly tortoise was the slowest animal on Earth," laughed Hare as he ran down the path.

All of a sudden Hare heard a lot of shouting. "What is that noise?" he wondered. He hurried down the path. There was Tortoise only a few feet from the finish line. The loud shouts Hare had heard were the sounds of the other animals cheering for Tortoise.

"Oh no! I can't let that pokey tortoise beat me," cried Hare. He ran as fast as he could, but it was too late. There was no way he could get to the finish line before Tortoise.

Hare may have been the faster runner, but Tortoise proved that slow and steady wins the race.

The Tortoise and the Hare

What Is the Moral?

Materials

- page 10, reproduced for each student

Steps to Follow

Follow these steps to help students complete the writing form. Use the same approach to help students complete a similar form in each of the other pockets.

❶ Distribute the writing form to students. Read aloud the definition of a moral. Point out that all fables have a moral.

❷ Ask students to recall the moral of "The Tortoise and the Hare." If they have difficulty recalling it, reread the last part of the fable aloud. Have students raise their hands when they hear the lesson learned. (You might also have students scan the story independently to find the moral.) Then write the moral on the chalkboard for students to copy onto their writing forms.

❸ Discuss the meaning of the moral. Have students write it in their own words on the form.

❹ Discuss how the moral applies to real life. Give examples from your own life. Have students work in small groups or individually to brainstorm examples of their own. Have them write one of those examples on the form.

❺ Invite students to share their examples with the rest of the class. Extend the activity by having students draw a picture to go with their example.

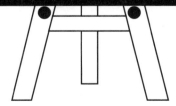

Moral—Slow and steady wins the race.

Meaning—Keep trying and you will succeed.

Example—My friend had trouble catching a ball, but she kept trying and trying until she could do it.

Name: _____

What Is the Moral?

A fable is a short story that teaches a lesson.
That lesson is called a moral.

Find the moral of "The Tortoise and the Hare." Write it here.

_____

_____

Explain what the moral means.

_____

_____

Give a real-life example of the moral. Tell about your own experience or about someone you know.

_____

_____

_____

_____

_____

_____

_____

_____

**The Tortoise
and the Hare**

The Winner!

Materials
- page 12, reproduced for each student
- real medals (optional)
- scissors
- 9" x 12" (23 x 30.5 cm) yellow construction paper
- crayons, colored pencils, marking pens
- hole punch
- 24" (61 cm) pieces of ribbon

Steps to Follow

❶ Discuss with students the purpose of a medal. Display real medals if you have them. Invite students to describe medals they have seen and tell why the medals were presented.

❷ Explain to students that they will create a medal for Tortoise for winning the race. On the chalkboard, write *"Awarded for _____,"* and ask students to suggest words that could be used to complete the statement about Tortoise. For example, *"Awarded for Never Giving Up."* List students' suggestions on the board.

❸ Guide students through the following steps to create a medal for Tortoise:

  a. Cut out the medal pattern.

  b. Lay the pattern on construction paper and trace it. Cut out the medal.

  c. Write on the medal the reason why Tortoise won the race. Begin with *"Awarded for."* You may choose words listed on the board.

  d. Color and decorate the medal. You may write other words or phrases on the back, such as *"The Winner!"* or *"Gold Medal."*

  e. Punch a hole in the top of the medal. String a ribbon through the hole. Tie the ends of the ribbon together.

❹ Extend the activity by having students write about an awards ceremony for Tortoise. Have them describe what happens during the event.

The Tortoise and the Hare

Medal Pattern

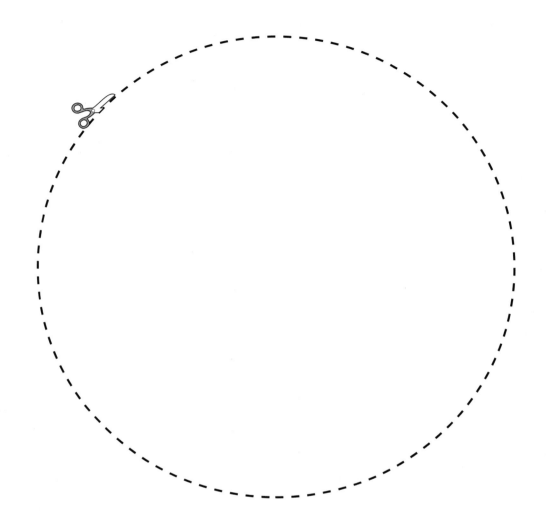

Describe the Tortoise and the Hare

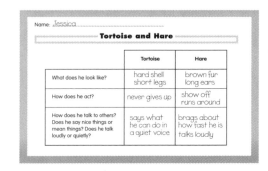

	Tortoise	Hare
Tortoise and Hare		
What does he look like?	hard shell short legs	brown fur long ears
How does he act?	never gives up	show off runs around
How does he talk to others? Does he say nice things or mean things? Does he talk loudly or quietly?	says what he can do in a quiet voice	brags about how fast he is talks loudly

Name: Jessica

Materials

- page 14, reproduced for each student
- overhead transparency of page 14
- overhead projector and markers
- crayons, colored pencils, marking pens
- scissors
- large index cards
- glue

Steps to Follow

❶ Use the transparency to review the writing form with students. Discuss the different ways to describe and compare the characters: by appearance, actions, and spoken words. Point out to students that what each character says and does can reveal a lot about that character's personality.

❷ Work together to complete the form, or have students work in small groups to complete the form independently. Encourage students to refer back to the descriptive words and illustrations in the story. Use the transparency to record answers for students to copy, or use it to record answers that groups share after everyone has completed the form.

❸ Have students color and cut out the pictures of Tortoise and Hare. Have them glue each picture onto the front of an index card. On the back of the card, have them write a paragraph describing that character.

❹ Ask questions such as the following to reinforce students' understanding of the characters. Students should respond to each question by holding up one or both of their picture cards. Invite students to give reasons for their choices.

- Which character moves quickly? Which character moves slowly?
- Which character speaks softly? Which character speaks loudly?
- Which character is a hard worker?
- Which character has a hard shell?
- Which character is unkind?
- Which character is confident and proud?
- Which character likes to talk about himself?
- Which character would be a good student?
- Which character would be a good friend?

The Tortoise and the Hare

Tortoise and Hare

	Tortoise	Hare
What does he look like?		
How does he act?		
How does he talk to others? Does he say nice things or mean things? Does he talk loudly or quietly?		

Materials

- writing paper
- 12" x 18" (30.5 x 45.5 cm) construction paper
- stapler
- crayons, colored pencils, marking pens
- drawing paper

Steps to Follow

❶ Ask students to recall the type of race described in the fable. Then work with students to brainstorm a list of other types of races that they have participated in or have seen (e.g., a bike race, a swim meet, a three-legged foot race).

❷ Guide students through the following steps to write a story about a real or make-believe race:

 a. Decide what type of race you want to write about. You may write about a real or make-believe race.

 b. Decide who is in the race. One racer can be you.

 c. Write a story about the race. Remember to tell:

> Who is in the race.
> Where the race takes place.
> When the race takes place.
> What happens during the race.
> How the race ends.

 d. Draw a picture to go with your story.

 e. Staple the story and the picture in a construction paper folder. Write the title and draw another picture on the cover.

❸ Have students read their stories aloud to a partner.

The Tortoise and the Hare

The Lion and the Mouse

Have students use these reproducibles to make The Lion and the Mouse pocket label and bookmark. (See page 2.)

The Story of
Share and discuss this fable about a tiny mouse who rescues a large lion. Reproduce the story on pages 19 and 20 for students. Use the teaching ideas on page 18 to preview, read, and review the story. Follow up with the "More to Explore" activities.

Use this reproducible to review the meaning of the fable's moral with students. Have students rewrite the moral in their own words and then apply it to real-life situations.

Using this poetic version of "The Lion and the Mouse" as a model, students write their own couplets about mice and other animals.

Students retell the story by sequencing picture cards and then writing about each illustrated event.

One Good Turn
Here's a chance for students to express their feelings about performing good deeds. Students write about their own good deeds and how it made them feel to help someone. Then they write about a good deed someone did for them and how it made them feel.

Using a small paper plate, plenty of string, and specific drawing instructions, students create a crafty portrait of the little mouse trying to rescue the trapped lion.

The Lion and the Mouse

Story characters:

Lion

Mouse

Moral of the story:

One good turn deserves another.

I liked this story:

☐ Yes

☐ No

This bookmark belongs to

_____

(your name)

Share The Lion and the Mouse

Preview the Story

State the title of the fable, and have students read aloud the names of the characters listed on the bookmark. Distribute copies of the fable (pages 19 and 20), and have students preview the pictures. Invite students who are unfamiliar with the fable to predict what happens when a mouse crosses paths with a lion.

Read the Story

Read the fable aloud as students follow along. Encourage students to track the text and underline or frame key words. List and discuss any unfamiliar words, such as *whiskers, jaw, critter, pitiful, plea, scurried, wail, repay,* and *worthwhile.* Point out picture clues and context clues that help explain parts of the fable. After you have read the fable aloud, encourage students to reread it independently or with a partner.

Review the Story

Ask questions such as the following to help students recall important details about the characters, setting, and plot of the fable:

- Who are the main characters of this fable?
- Where does the story take place?
- How did the mouse get caught by the lion?
- Why did the lion think that the mouse couldn't help him?
- Why do you think the lion let the mouse go?
- How did the mouse help the lion?

More to Explore

- Opposites

  Prompt students to use words with opposite meanings to compare the lion and the mouse. For example: *large, small; loud, quiet; scared, brave; fat, skinny; hungry, full.* List those words on a T-chart comparing the lion and the mouse.

- What Does It Mean?

  Have students scan the story to locate a word that means about the same thing as each of these words:

hand *(paw)*	beg *(plea)*	frightened *(scared)*
nice *(kind)*	animal *(critter)*	foolish *(silly)*
ran *(scurried)*	shout *(cry)*	tiny *(little, small)*

The Lion and the Mouse

The Lion and the Mouse

A hungry little mouse didn't happen to see
A large old lion resting under a tree.

The mouse climbed over the lion's paw,
And tripped on whiskers near the lion's jaw.

Down came the paw on the mouse's tail.
The mouse felt like she was trapped in jail.

The poor little critter was so scared she shook,
As the lion stared down with a terrible look.

"Oh, please," begged the mouse with a pitiful plea.
"Please, good lion, don't eat me."

The little mouse cried, "Won't you set me free?
Someday I'll help you. Just you wait and see."

The big old lion laughed at the mouse's words.
"That's the silliest thing I've ever heard."

He said, "How can a mouse so weak and skinny
Ever help someone as large as me?"

But the lion wasn't hungry, and the mouse was so small.
"Today's your lucky day. I won't eat you after all."

The mouse took off running, "You're very kind."
She didn't wait for the lion to change his mind.

The next day, the mouse heard the lion's cry.
"That's the lion crying. I wonder why?"

The mouse scurried toward that terrible wail.
She found the lion trapped from nose to tail.

"Don't worry, lion. I'm here to save you."
And the brave little mouse began to chew.

Before he could believe it, the old lion was free.
The little mouse danced and laughed with glee.

"I told you I'd repay your kindness someday.
I just didn't know it would be this way."

"Thank you, good mouse," said the lion with a smile.
"I see now that kindness is always worthwhile."

The moral of the story: *One good turn deserves another.*

**The Lion and
the Mouse**

Name: _____

What Is the Moral?

A fable is a short story that teaches a lesson.
That lesson is called a moral.

Find the moral of "The Lion and the Mouse." Write it here.

_____

_____

Explain what the moral means.

_____

_____

Give a real-life example of the moral. Tell about your own experience or about someone you know.

_____

_____

_____

_____

_____

_____

_____

_____

**The Lion and
the Mouse**

Rhyme Time

Materials
- drawing paper
- crayons, colored pencils, marking pens

Steps to Follow

❶ Reread the fable aloud or have students reread it silently. Point out that the fable is written as a poem with couplets—pairs of lines that rhyme. Ask students to find the rhyming words in each couplet. List the words on the chalkboard as students underline them in the fable.

❷ Ask students to say other rhyming words for each couplet. For example: *A hungry little mouse didn't happen to see…a large old lion resting under a tree (bee, flea, key, ski).*

❸ Have students write their own couplets about a mouse or another animal. Guide them through the following steps to model the process. Be sure students understand that a couplet may be two complete sentences or one sentence divided into two parts. Encourage more advanced students to write a full-length poem of couplets.

a. Select an animal. Write the first line of your couplet.

A mouse named Pat

b. Make a list of words that rhyme with the last word.

bat	cat	fat	hat	gnat	mat	rat	sat

c. Think of a second line that ends with one of those rhyming words.

Saw a big mean cat. Lived in a tall black hat. Was in love with a rat.

d. Write the first and second lines on a sheet of drawing paper.

A mouse named Pat Was in love with a rat.

e. Draw a picture to go with your couplet. Or write more couplets about the animal and then draw the picture.

Sequence and Write the Story

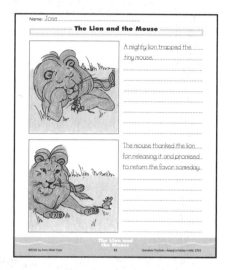
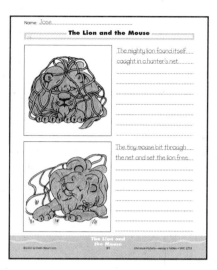

Materials

- page 24, reproduced for each student
- page 25, two copies reproduced for each student
- crayons, colored pencils, marking pens
- scissors
- glue
- stapler

Steps to Follow

❶ Ask students to recall events from the story. Prompt them to list the events in the correct sequence as you write their responses on the chalkboard.

❷ Guide students through the following steps to complete the sequencing activity:

a. Color and cut out the pictures.

b. Glue them in order in the boxes.

c. Write about what is happening in each picture to retell the story.

❸ Staple each student's pages together. Have students read aloud their descriptions to a partner.

The Lion and the Mouse

24

The Lion and the Mouse

paste

_____
_____
_____
_____
_____
_____
_____
_____

paste

_____
_____
_____
_____
_____
_____
_____
_____

**The Lion and
the Mouse**

One Good Turn Deserves Another

Materials
- page 27, reproduced for each student
- crayons, colored pencils, marking pens
- scissors
- 9" x 12" (23 x 30.5 cm) construction paper

Steps to Follow

❶ Discuss the phrase "One good turn deserves another" with students. Give an example from your own life.

❷ Draw a T-chart on the chalkboard and label the two columns as shown. Ask students to share examples for each column as you record their responses. Invite volunteers to share their feelings about helping others or receiving help from others.

Someone helped me.	I helped someone

❸ Have students cut out the pattern, trace it onto construction paper, and cut out the paper doll. Guide them through the following steps to complete the activity:

a. On one side of the paper doll, name someone who helped you. Write about what that person did for you. Write about how you felt.

b. On the other side of the paper doll, name someone you helped. Write about what you did for that person. Write about how you felt.

c. Draw your own face on both sides of the paper doll.

Paper Doll Pattern

27 Literature Pockets—Aesop's Fables • EMC 2733

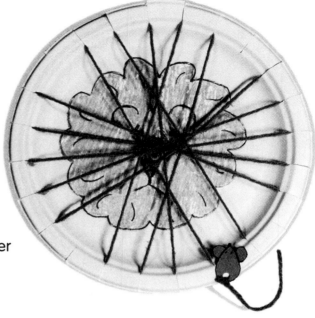

Materials

- small paper plates
- crayons, colored pencils, marking pens
- scissors
- 36" (91.5 cm) pieces of string, three for each student
- tape
- 2" x 3" (5 x 7.5 cm) gray construction paper
- hole punch

Steps to Follow

❶ Show students how to draw a lion in the center of a plate. Follow these steps:

❷ After students draw the lion, guide them through the following steps:

a. Cut slits around the edge of the plate. Cut them about 1" (2.5 cm) apart.

b. Wrap the string back and forth around the plate to form a "net" in front of the lion. Cut off a small piece of string from one of the ends to use for the mouse's tail (later on). Tape the ends of the string to the back of the plate.

c. Draw a little mouse on gray construction paper.

d. Cut out the mouse. Punch a hole in the tail end of the mouse and tie on the small piece of string for the tail.

e. Tape the mouse onto the edge of the plate to show it chewing the net.

The Lion and the Mouse

The Boy Who Cried Wolf

Have students use these reproducibles to make
The Boy Who Cried Wolf pocket label and bookmark.
(See page 2.)

Share and discuss this fable about a mischievous boy
who cries "Wolf!" one time too many. Reproduce the
story on pages 32 and 33 for students. Use the teaching
ideas on page 31 to preview, read, and review the story.
Follow up with the "More to Explore" activities.

Use this reproducible to review the meaning of the
fable's moral with students. Have students rewrite the
moral in their own words and then apply it to real-life
situations.

With just a few pieces of torn paper, students make an
adorable flock of sheep. Then they write about how they
would protect their sheep from a hungry wolf.

After learning the meanings of special words from the
story, students make a little picture dictionary to show
what they know.

Students assemble a three-dimensional pop-out face
of a shepherd boy who announces, "I'm bored!" Then
they list activities that the shepherd boy could have done
instead of trying to fool the villagers.

Students color, cut, and fold to make a little nonfiction
book about wool. Read the book together. Bring in
samples of wool yarn, wool fabric, and sheared wool
(if possible) to share with the class.

The Boy Who Cried Wolf

Story characters:

 Shepherd Boy

 Wolf

 Flock of Sheep

 Villagers

Moral of the story:

No one believes a liar, even when he is telling the truth.

I liked this story:

☐ Yes

☐ No

This bookmark belongs to

_____

(your name)

Share The Boy Who Cried Wolf

Preview the Story

State the title of the fable, and have students read aloud the names of the characters listed on the bookmark. Distribute copies of the fable (pages 32 and 33), and have students preview the pictures. Invite students who are unfamiliar with the fable to predict what happens when a boy lies about seeing a wolf.

Read the Story

Read the fable aloud as students follow along. Encourage students to track the text and underline or frame key words. List and discuss any unfamiliar words, such as *wander, bored, stared, fool, pitchforks, clubs, crept, ignored, drove,* and *liar.* Point out picture clues and context clues that help explain parts of the fable. After you have read the fable aloud, encourage students to reread it independently or with a partner.

Review the Story

Ask questions such as the following to help students recall important details about the characters, setting, and plot of the fable:

- What was the shepherd boy's job?
- Why was he bored?
- What trick did he play on the villagers?
- Why didn't the villagers come when a wolf really showed up?
- What do you think happened to the shepherd boy? Why?
- Why do you think people sometimes tell lies?

More to Explore

- Trust

  Lead the class in a discussion of ways the shepherd boy might win back the trust of the villagers. Extend the activity by asking students to select the way they feel would be most successful and write about it.

- Facial Expressions

  Explain to students that facial expressions reveal a lot about what a person is thinking and feeling. Have students draw faces that show the shepherd boy's thoughts and feelings during different parts of the story: watching the sheep; deciding to fool the villagers; seeing the villagers run up the hill; seeing the wolf creep toward the flock, realizing that no one is coming to help.

The Boy
Who Cried Wolf

The Boy Who Cried Wolf

There once was a shepherd boy who was in charge of his family's flock of sheep. Every morning he took the sheep to a meadow near the village. All day long he watched the sheep. He had to make sure they were safe. He had to make sure they did not wander off or get eaten by other animals.

The shepherd boy grew tired of his job. "I'm bored," he said. "There is nothing to do but watch these silly sheep eat grass. Nothing different ever happens."

As the shepherd boy stared unhappily at the sheep in the meadow, he had an idea. "Wouldn't it be fun to fool the villagers?" he thought. "I'll pretend that a wolf is attacking the flock of sheep."

32

The shepherd boy shouted, "Wolf! Wolf!" The villagers came running. They brought pitchforks and clubs to scare off the wolf. But when they reached the meadow, there was no wolf. There was just the shepherd boy laughing at them.

Again and again, the shepherd boy cried wolf. Again and again, the villagers came. Each time there was no wolf.

At last, one day, a hungry wolf crept up on the flock. When the shepherd boy saw the wolf, he cried out, "Wolf! Wolf!"

He shouted and shouted, but no one came. The villagers thought that he was up to his old tricks. They just ignored his calls. The wolf killed many sheep before the shepherd boy drove it away.

The shepherd boy finally learned his lesson. No one believes a liar, even when he is telling the truth.

Name: _____

What Is the Moral?

A fable is a short story that teaches a lesson.
That lesson is called a moral.

Find the moral of "The Boy Who Cried Wolf." Write it here.

_____

_____

Explain what the moral means.

_____

_____

Give a real-life example of the moral. Tell about your own experience or about someone you know.

_____

_____

_____

_____

_____

_____

_____

_____

**The Boy
Who Cried Wolf**

A Flock of Sheep

Materials

- construction paper for each sheep:
    - 3" x 4" (7.5 x 10 cm) piece of white construction paper—body
    - 2" (5 cm) square of white construction paper—head
    - 2" (5 cm) square of black construction paper—legs and ears
- 6" x 9" (15 x 23 cm) piece of green construction paper—grass
- 12" x 18" (30.5 x 45.5 cm) sheets of blue construction paper—backing
- scissors
- glue
- black marking pen
- writing paper
- clear tape

Steps to Follow

❶ Guide students through the following steps to make one sheep. Then have them make two or three more sheep on the same paper to finish the flock:

a. Tear the white pieces of paper to make the sheep's body and head as shown. Tear the tail out of a scrap of white paper. Glue the parts together on a sheet of blue construction paper.

b. Fold and cut the black paper in half. Cut one piece in half the long way to make two legs. Glue the legs onto the sheep's body (side view).

c. Fold the other piece of black paper in half. Cut out two ears. Glue them onto the sheep's head.

d. Use a black marking pen to draw the sheep's eyes, nose, and mouth.

e. Cut the edges of the green paper to make a patch of grass. Glue the grass under the sheep's feet.

❷ After students complete their flock of sheep, have them pretend to be the shepherd boy. Ask them to write a paragraph telling how they would protect their flock from a hungry wolf. Have them tape the paragraph onto the back of their picture.

Note: Fold the picture in half to fit it inside the pocket.

The Boy Who Cried Wolf

A Picture Dictionary

Materials

- page 37, two copies reproduced for each student
- crayons, colored pencils, marking pens
- scissors
- 4" x 6" (10 x 15 cm) construction paper
- hole punch
- metal rings

Steps to Follow

❶ Display the following words: *shepherd, flock, village, meadow, pitchfork, wolf.* Point to each word and review its meaning with students. Encourage students to use context clues from the story to figure out word meanings.

❷ Guide students through the following steps to make a picture dictionary of the listed words:

a. Cut the six forms apart. Fold each one on the fold line.

b. Write one word on the front of each folded section.

c. Draw a picture in the box to illustrate the word.

d. Unfold each form. On the lines, write a sentence that includes the word.

e. Punch holes in the upper left-hand corner of the forms and the construction paper cover pieces. (Locate the correct spot on the cover by using one of the pages as a guide.) Use a metal ring to fasten the pages and the cover together.

f. On the front cover, write "_____'s *Picture Dictionary.*" Write your name in the blank.

The Boy Who Cried Wolf

I'm Bored!

Materials

- page 39, reproduced for each student
- crayons, colored pencils, marking pens
- scissors
- scraps of construction paper
- glue
- 9" x 12" (23 x 30.5 cm) construction paper
- 5" x 8" (13 x 20 cm) writing paper

Steps to Follow

❶ Guide students through the following steps to make a pop-out face. (You may need to help younger students push the nose and mouth into position.)

   a. Color the shepherd boy's face.

   b. Fold the form in half and cut along the marked lines.

   c. Fold the nose and mouth as shown. Push them through to the front of the face.

   d. Cut out the face. Glue on some hair made from paper scraps.

   e. Fold a sheet of construction paper in half. Put glue on the back of one half of the face. Fit the folded edge of the face snugly into the fold of the construction paper so that the back of the face sticks to the paper. Leave some space below the face. Rub the top of the face to secure it in place. Then put glue on the back of the other half of the face and secure it in place.

   f. Cut out the speech bubbles and glue them on either side of the shepherd boy's face. Fold and open the construction paper to see his mouth and nose pop out.

❷ After students finish the shepherd boy's face, review what the shepherd boy did when he got bored. Ask students to suggest other activities the shepherd boy could have done to keep himself busy. Have them list their ideas on a strip of writing paper and then glue the strip below the shepherd boy's face.

39

Note: Reproduce this page for each student. Use the directions on page 29 to help students complete the activity.

1

What Is Wool?

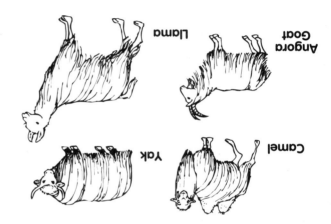

Merino

Wool is a special kind of fur. Most wool comes from sheep. There are many different kinds of sheep. The best wool comes from Merino sheep. Their wool, or fleece, is fine and thick.

4

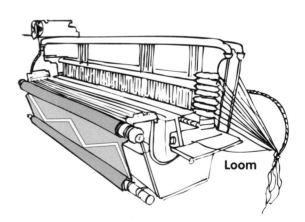

Angora Goat

Llama

Yak

Camel

Sheep are not the only animals that give wool. They are just easier to raise than many other long-haired animals. Camels, yaks, goats, and llamas also provide wool that is used to make cloth.

fold 2

fold 1

2

Sheep have their wool cut off in late spring or early summer. This is called shearing. Today this is usually done with electric clippers. The shearers work fast, but carefully. They don't want to cut the sheep. They try to get the whole fleece off in one piece.

3

Loom

The wool is washed several times. Then it is combed (carded) to untangle it. The wool is spun into fine threads called yarn. The yarn is woven into cloth on a loom.

The Miller, His Son, and Their Donkey

Pocket Label and Bookmark .... **page 42**
Have students use these reproducibles to make The Miller, His Son, and Their Donkey pocket label and bookmark. (See page 2.)

The Story of The Miller, His Son, and Their Donkey .... **pages 43–45**
Share and discuss this fable about a miller who learns that you can't please everyone. Reproduce the story on pages 44 and 45 for students. Use the teaching ideas on page 43 to preview, read, and review the story. Follow up with the "More to Explore" activities.

What Is the Moral? .... **page 46**
Use this reproducible to review the meaning of the fable's moral with students. Have students rewrite the moral in their own words and then apply it to real-life situations.

A Storyboard Set .... **pages 47 and 48**
Students use prop-up characters on a tabletop setting to retell the fable.

Grinding Wheat .... **pages 49 and 50**
Have you ever wondered how wheat and other grains have been ground into flour throughout the years? Students assemble an illustrated minibook about the different methods. Read and discuss the facts with students.

The Miller, His Son, and Their Donkey

Story characters:

 Miller

 Son

 Donkey

 Old Men

 Old Women

Moral of the story:

If you try to please everyone, you'll please no one, not even yourself.

I liked this story:

☐ Yes

☐ No

This bookmark belongs to

_____

(your name)

Share The Miller, His Son, and Their Donkey

Preview the Story

State the title of the fable, and have students read aloud the names of the characters listed on the bookmark. Distribute copies of the fable (pages 44 and 45), and have students preview the pictures. Invite students who are unfamiliar with the fable to predict what happens when the miller and his son go to the market with their donkey.

Read the Story

Read the fable aloud as students follow along. Encourage students to track the text and underline or frame key words. List and discuss any unfamiliar words, such as *drought*, *crop*, *ground*, *respect*, *lazy*, *comfort*, *overloaded*, and *cruel*. Point out picture clues and context clues that help explain parts of the fable. After you read the fable aloud, encourage students to reread it independently or with a partner.

Review the Story

Ask questions such as the following to help students recall important details about the characters, setting, and plot of the fable:

- Why was the miller going to sell the donkey?
- What advice did the miller get from the farmer? the old man? the old woman?
- Why were the people at the bridge mad at the miller and his son?
- How did the donkey end up in the river?
- What words would you use to describe the miller? Why?
- What lesson did the miller learn?

More to Explore

- The Best Way

    Review the ways the miller and his son used the donkey. (one rode it, they both rode it, neither rode it, they carried it) Ask students to decide which they think is the best way to use the donkey. Have them write an explanation and draw a picture to go with their writing.

- Kinds of Work

    The miller ground wheat into flour to earn money for his family. As a class or in small groups, have students brainstorm a list of other kinds of work that people do to earn money. Have them choose which kind of work they would like to do and write about why they would like to do it.

The Miller, His Son,
and Their Donkey

The Miller, His Son, and Their Donkey

It had been a bad year for farmers. There was a drought, and the wheat crop was small. Only a few farmers brought wheat to the mill to be ground into flour. The miller needed money to feed his family. "Since I can't make enough money grinding flour," he told his family, "I will have to sell our donkey."

The next morning, the miller and his son set out for the market to sell the donkey. As they walked along the dusty road, they passed a farmer working in his field. The man laughed at the miller and his son. "What fools you are!" he shouted. "Why do you walk on such a hot day when one of you could ride that donkey?"

"That's a good idea," said the miller. He lifted his young son onto the donkey's back and they headed down the road.

Soon they passed a group of old men resting beside the road. "Look at that!" said one of the old men. "Children have no respect these days. That lazy boy rides while his poor father has to walk in the dust."

"That old man might be right," thought the miller. His son climbed down off the donkey's back. The miller got on and they started down the road again.

A mile down the road, the miller and his son passed a group of old women gathering apples from a tree. "Shame on you!" said one of the old women. "How can you ride in comfort while your poor son has to walk? Can't you see how tired he is?"

The miller thought about what the old woman had said. "You do look tired, Son. Climb up behind me. We will both ride to market."

Not far from town, the miller and his son rode past a crowd of people standing by a bridge. The crowd pointed and shouted at the miller and his son. "That poor donkey is overloaded carrying both of you. How can you be so cruel!"

The miller and his son tried to think of what to do. At last they decided to carry the donkey so it could get some rest. They cut down a pole and tied the donkey's feet to it. They tried to carry the donkey across the bridge, but the donkey was too heavy. They dropped the donkey and it fell off the bridge and into the water.

As the miller and his son jumped into the water to save their donkey, the miller told his son, "That will teach us to try to please everyone. We have pleased no one, not even ourselves."

The Miller, His Son, and Their Donkey

Name: _____

What Is the Moral?

A fable is a short story that teaches a lesson.
That lesson is called a moral.

Find the moral of "The Miller, His Son, and Their Donkey." Write it here.

_____

_____

Explain what the moral means.

_____

_____

Give a real-life example of the moral. Tell about your own experience or about someone you know.

_____

_____

_____

_____

_____

_____

_____

_____

**The Miller, His Son,
and Their Donkey**

A Storyboard Set

Materials

- page 48, reproduced for each student
- 12" x 18" (30.5 x 45.5 cm) construction paper
- crayons, colored pencils, marking pens
- scissors
- glue
- clear tape
- five 5" x 1" (13 x 2.5 cm) strips of construction paper for stands
- 3½" x 5" (9 x 13 cm) brown construction paper for bridge
- legal-sized envelopes
- 7" (18 cm) pieces of pipe cleaner

Steps to Follow

Guide students through the following steps to make a storyboard about the fable:

❶ On the sheet of construction paper, draw a river across the paper from top to bottom as shown.

❷ Glue the brown paper across the river for a bridge as shown.

❸ Draw a road across the paper from the left edge to the bridge and from the right side of the bridge to the right edge of the paper as shown.

❹ On each side of the road, draw details such as apple trees, fields of wheat, and so on.

❺ Tape an envelope to the back of the storyboard.

❻ Color and cut out all of the characters. Fold the construction paper strips in half and glue them onto the back of the miller, his son, donkey #1, the old men, and the old women for stands for stands. Trim off any brown paper that shows around the edges.

❼ Cut slits in the miller and his son as marked. This allows the characters to slide onto the back of the donkey when they are supposed to be riding it.

❽ Cut both slits in donkey #2. Slide the pipe cleaner through the legs. Bend each end of the pipe cleaner to make two little hooks. Slide the hooks around the necks of the miller and his son.

❾ Move the characters on the storyboard to retell the fable.

❿ When you are done, store the pieces in the envelope on the back of the storyboard.

The Miller, His Son, and Their Donkey

Story Characters

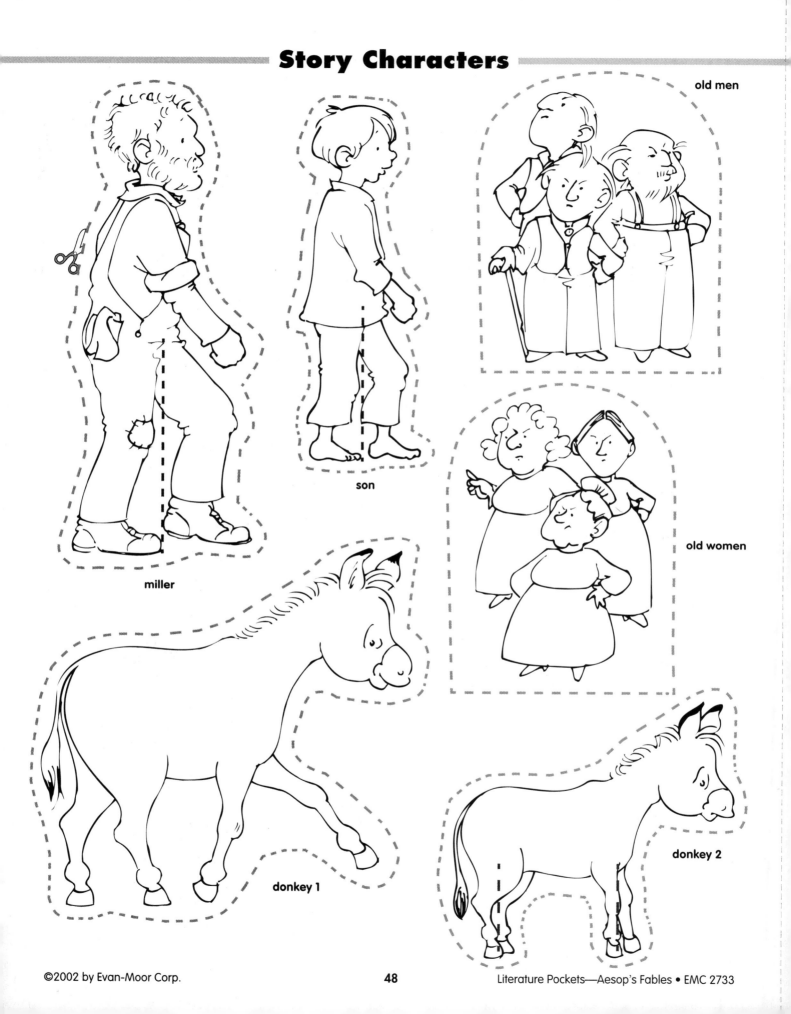

old men

son

old women

miller

donkey 1

donkey 2

48

Grinding Wheat

Thousands of years ago, wheat and other seeds were ground into flour by using a large stone and a small stone.

Hundreds of years ago, horses were used to turn a wheel to grind wheat into flour.

In some countries, wind or water was used to turn wheels to grind wheat into flour.

Today, large machines use electricity to turn the wheels that grind wheat into flour.

Materials
- page 50, reproduced for each student
- overhead transparency of page 50
- overhead projector
- 4" x 18" (10 x 45.5 cm) construction paper
- crayons, colored pencils, marking pens
- scissors
- glue

Steps to Follow

❶ Project the overhead transparency as the class reads and discusses what is shown.

❷ Give each student a strip of construction paper. Show students how to fold the paper into fourths and refold it accordion style.

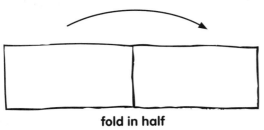

fold in half

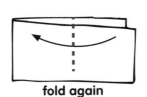

fold again

open and fold accordion style

❸ Have students color, cut out, and glue the picture cards in correct sequence onto the sections of the accordion-folded paper. Have them refold the sections and write the title *"Grinding Wheat"* on the outside of the first section.

❹ Have students read their accordion books aloud or to a partner.

The Miller, His Son, and Their Donkey

Grinding Wheat

1 Thousands of years ago, wheat and other seeds were ground into flour by using a large stone and a small stone.

3 In some countries, wind or water was used to turn wheels to grind wheat into flour.

2 Hundreds of years ago, horses were used to turn a wheel to grind wheat into flour.

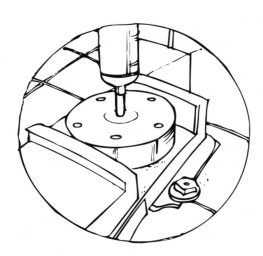

4 Today, large machines use electricity to turn the wheels that grind wheat into flour.

The Milkmaid and Her Pail

The Milkmaid and Her Pail

Story characters:

Milkmaid

Cow

Mother

Moral of the story:

Don't count your chickens before they are hatched.

I liked this story:

☐ Yes

☐ No

This bookmark belongs to

_____

(your name)

The Milkmaid and Her Pail

Share The Milkmaid and Her Pail

Preview the Story

State the title of the fable, and have students read aloud the names of the characters listed on the bookmark. Distribute copies of the fable (pages 54 and 55), and have students preview the pictures. Invite students who are unfamiliar with the fable to predict what happens to the milkmaid's pail and why.

Read the Story

Read the fable aloud as students follow along. Encourage students to track the text and underline or frame key words. List and discuss any unfamiliar words, such as *milked, cowshed, munch, market, balanced, daydream, cream, churn, flock, wildflowers,* and *playfully.* Point out picture clues and context clues that help explain parts of the fable. After you have read the fable aloud, encourage students to reread it independently or with a partner.

Review the Story

Ask questions such as the following to help students recall important details about the characters, setting, and plot of the fable:

- Who is Millie? Where does she live and what does she do?
- The fable says that Millie was daydreaming. What is a daydream?
- What did Millie plan to do with the cream from the milk? Name all of her ideas.
- What happened to ruin Millie's plans?
- What caused the pail to fall off Millie's head?
- What do you think Millie learned from her experience?

More to Explore

- Compound Words

  Review compound words with students. Use the word *milkmaid* as an example. Then have students scan the story to find other compound words. *(cowshed, farmhouse, daydream, anything, wildflowers, alongside)* List those words on the chalkboard. Have students copy them on paper and draw a line between the first and second word in each compound. Extend the lesson by asking students to illustrate the compound words or to think of other ones to add to the list.

- Earn and Spend Money

  Remind students that Millie wanted to earn enough money to buy a pretty dress. Ask students to think of something that they would like to buy. (Encourage them to think of something they could really use.) Have them draw the item and then write about how they might earn enough money to buy it.

**The Milkmaid
and Her Pail**

The Milkmaid and Her Pail

The family's cow had to be milked every day. Millie, the oldest daughter, did this job. She got up early and headed for the cowshed. She gave the cow a big handful of hay to munch on while being milked. "Swish, swish, swish" went the warm milk into the pail. Usually the milk was for the family to drink. But on market day, Millie was allowed to keep the milk and sell it.

Today was market day. Millie quickly finished milking the cow. She balanced the pail of fresh, sweet milk on her head and started walking back to the farmhouse. As she walked, she began to daydream.

"This is good, rich milk," Millie thought. "It will have plenty of cream. I will churn the cream into fresh white butter to sell at the market. After I sell the butter, I'll buy a dozen eggs for hatching. Soon I'll have a flock of chickens running around the yard. When they are grown, I'll sell the chickens for a good price."

Millie was so busy daydreaming, she did not notice anything else. She didn't see the wildflowers growing alongside the road. She didn't hear the birds singing in the trees. "With that money, I'll buy myself a beautiful new dress to wear to the fair in the summer," she thought. "I'll look so pretty in that dress that the miller's son will beg me to marry him. But will I? Never!"

As she thought about the miller's son, Millie tossed her head playfully. Down fell the pail off her head. The milk spilled all over the ground. And so the milkmaid had nothing—no milk, no butter, no eggs, no chickens, and no new dress!

When she got home, Millie had to tell her mother what had happened. "Well, my child," said her mother as she gave Millie a hug, "I hope you have learned not to count your chickens before they are hatched."

The Milkmaid and Her Pail

Name: _____

What Is the Moral?

A fable is a short story that teaches a lesson.
That lesson is called a moral.

Find the moral of "The Milkmaid and Her Pail." Write it here.

_____

_____

Explain what the moral means.

_____

_____

Give a real-life example of the moral. Tell about your own experience or about someone you know.

_____

_____

_____

_____

_____

_____

_____

_____

**The Milkmaid
and Her Pail**

The Milkmaid's Daydreams

Name ___Jill___
cream
butter
eggs
chicken
dress
the miller's son

Millie and the Daydream Wheel

Materials
- page 58, reproduced for each student
- crayons, colored pencils, marking pens
- pointed scissors
- glue
- 4" (10 cm) square of construction paper
- brass paper fasteners

Steps to Follow

❶ Guide students through the following steps to assemble a daydream wheel for Millie the milkmaid:

  a. Color and cut out Millie and the daydream wheel. Glue the wheel onto the square of construction paper. Cut out the wheel again.

  b. Cut out the opening in Millie's thought bubble. (Younger students may need help with this step.)

  c. Use a paper fastener to attach the wheel to the back of the thought bubble.

  d. On the lined section of the form, write the names of the illustrated objects. You may choose to have students practice using those words in sentences.

❷ Have students retell the fable to classmates or younger students at school as they turn the wheel to show each part of Millie's daydream.

❸ Extend the activity by having students write a paragraph on the back of the wheel about what happened when Millie tossed her head.

fold

Name _____

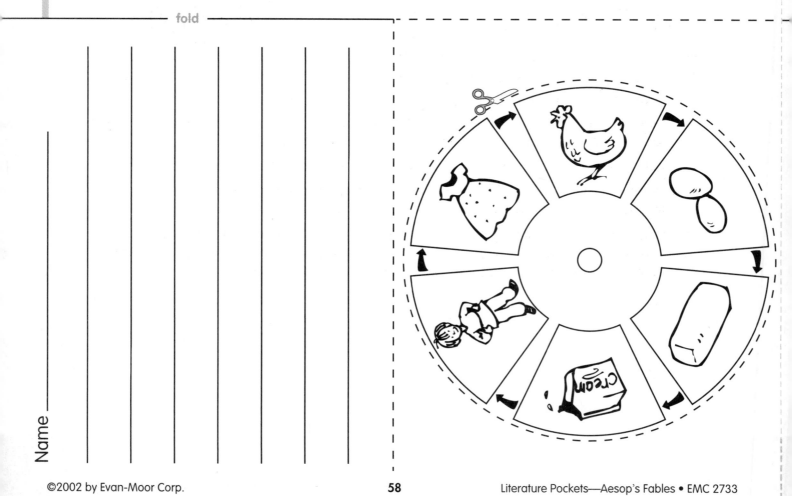

Cream to Butter

Materials
- page 60, reproduced for each student
- food jar with lid for each group of 6 students
- cream
- sink or container for liquid waste
- crackers
- plastic knives
- seasonings such as salt, honey, cinnamon, and vanilla extract (optional)

Steps to Follow

❶ Give each group a jar half full of cream. Be sure the lid is on tight. Ask students to predict how the cream will be changed into butter.

❷ Review the record sheet with students. Have them write a description of the cream in the "Before" section of the form.

❸ Guide students through the following steps to make butter:

  a. Taking turns, shake the jar 100 times. Look at the contents of the jar. If it is still liquid, shake the jar another 100 times.

  b. When a lump of butter has formed in the jar, complete the "What I Did" section of the form. Explain what you did to change the cream into butter.

  c. Pour any liquid out of the jar. Spread some of the butter on a cracker and taste it.

  d. Complete the "After" section of the form. Describe the changes that have occurred to the cream. Tell what you did after the cream turned into butter.

❹ Extend the activity by having students flavor some of their butter with salt or other seasonings (e.g., honey, cinnamon, vanilla extract) and compare the flavors. Encourage students to research how butter is made in large quantities for retail.

Cream to Butter

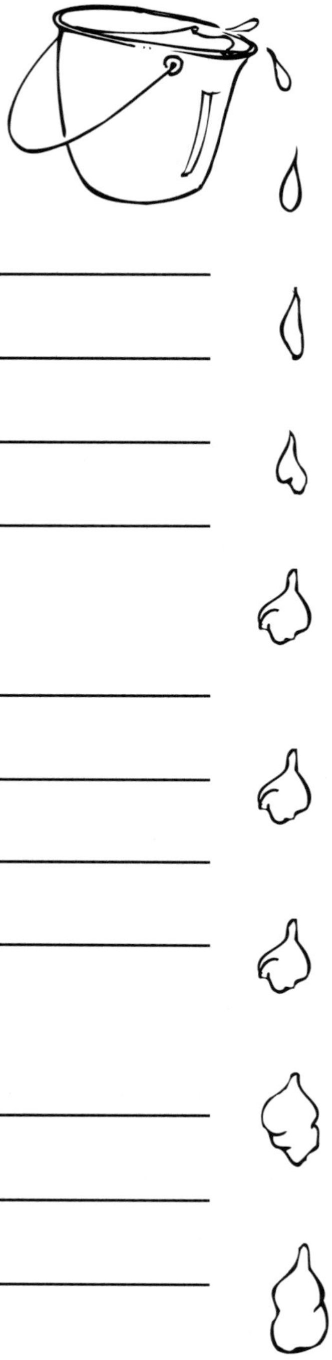

Before:

_____

_____

_____

What I Did:

_____

_____

_____

After:

_____

_____

_____

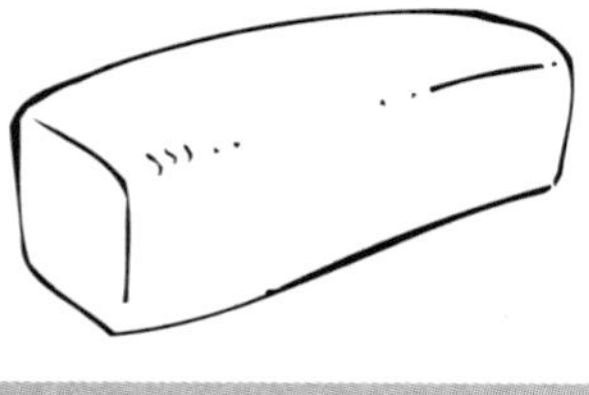

The Milkmaid and Her Pail

Name: _____

Spilled Milk

Pretend you are Millie and that you have spilled the milk.
How would you feel about spilling the milk?

_____

_____

_____

What would you say to your mother?

_____

_____

_____

Pretend you are Millie's mother and that Millie has spilled the milk.
What would you say to Millie?

_____

_____

_____

Why would you say that?

_____

_____

_____

**The Milkmaid
and Her Pail**

The Fox and the Goat

Pocket Label and Bookmark .... page 63
Have students use these reproducibles to make The Fox and the Goat pocket label and bookmark. (See page 2.)

The Story of
The Fox and the Goat .... pages 64–66
Share and discuss this fable about a sly fox who tricks a goat into helping him escape from a well. Reproduce the story on pages 65 and 66 for students. Use the teaching ideas on page 64 to preview, read, and review the story. Follow up with the "More to Explore" activities.

What Is the Moral? .... page 67
Use this reproducible to review the meaning of the fable's moral with students. Have students rewrite the moral in their own words and then apply it to real-life situations.

Down the Well .... pages 68 and 69
Students create a pull-through picture strip to show and tell what happened to both the fox and the goat.

Look Before You Leap .... pages 70 and 71
Students apply their understanding of the moral by creating a foldout minibook that illustrates the importance of looking before you leap.

Alike and Different .... page 72
What realistic traits do the fox and the goat possess? Students use this activity sheet to compare the similarities and differences between the fabled animals and their real counterparts. Use a transparency of the sheet to guide students through the activity.

The Fox and the Goat

Story characters:

 Mrs. Fox

 Mr. Goat

Moral of the story:

Look before you leap.

I liked this story:

☐ Yes

☐ No

This bookmark belongs to

_____

(your name)

The Fox and the Goat

Share The Fox and the Goat

Preview the Story

State the title of the fable, and have students read aloud the names of the characters listed on the bookmark. Distribute copies of the fable (pages 65 and 66), and have students preview the pictures. Invite students who are unfamiliar with the fable to predict what happens to the fox and the goat.

Read the Story

Read the fable aloud as students follow along. Encourage students to track the text and underline or frame key words. List and discuss any unfamiliar words, such as *stream*, *pond*, *leaned*, *unable*, *moaning*, *sly*, *foolish*, and *hooves*. Point out picture clues and context clues that help explain parts of the fable. After you have read the fable aloud, encourage students to reread it independently or with a partner.

Review the Story

Ask questions such as the following to help students recall important details about the characters, setting, and plot of the fable:

- How did the fox and goat end up in the well?
- Why do you think the animals couldn't get out of the well?
- What trick did the fox play on the goat?
- What do you think about the way the fox treated the goat?
- What do you think the goat will do the next time he sees the fox in trouble?

More to Explore

- A Way Out

  Divide the class into small groups. Challenge them to think of a way for Mr. Goat to get out of the well. Have each group member draw a picture or write a paragraph to explain the group's plan. Allow time for groups to share their ideas with the rest of the class.

- Plural Forms

  Review regular and irregular plural forms using words from the story as models. Write these words on the board: *day*, *fox*, *pond*, *goat*, *hoof*, *side*, *brain*. Have students fold a sheet of paper in half and copy the words from the chalkboard onto the left side of the paper. Have them write the plural form of each word on the right.

The Fox and the Goat

The Fox
and the Goat

One very hot summer day, a thirsty fox went looking for something to drink. She looked and looked for a stream or a pond where she could drink. At long last she saw a well in the distance.

The fox hurried to the well and leaned over to drink. Unfortunately, she leaned too far. Down she fell into the deep well. The fox was not hurt, but she was unable to climb out again.

As the fox sat at the bottom of the well, moaning about her bad luck, along came a goat. The thirsty goat looked into the well. "Oh my goodness, Mrs. Fox!" said the goat. "What are you doing sitting in the well?"

The sly fox answered, "I'm enjoying the water in this well, Mr. Goat. It is so cool and sweet. Why don't you join me."

The foolish goat jumped down into the well and took a big drink. "You were right, Mrs. Fox," he said. "This is wonderful water."

 Literature Pockets—Aesop's Fables • EMC 2733

Now that he was no longer thirsty, the goat looked for a way to get out of the well. "Oh no!" he cried. "How are we going to get out of the well?"

"I have an idea, Mr. Goat," said the sly fox. "Put your front hooves as high up the side of the well as you can. Then I will climb up your back to get out of the well." And that is just what the fox did.

"Now help me get out," said the goat.

But the fox just left him in the well. As she ran away, the fox called out, "If you had half as many brains as you have hairs in your beard, you would have looked before you leaped. Now find your own way out."

Name: _____

What Is the Moral?

A fable is a short story that teaches a lesson.
That lesson is called a moral.

Find the moral of "The Fox and the Goat." Write it here.

_____

_____

Explain what the moral means.

_____

_____

Give a real-life example of the moral. Tell about your own experience or about someone you know.

_____

_____

_____

_____

_____

_____

_____

_____

**The Fox and
the Goat**

Down the Well

Materials

- page 69, reproduced on light brown or gray construction paper for each student
- crayons, colored pencils, marking pens
- pointed scissors
- 4" x 18" (10 x 45.5 cm) strips of white construction paper

Steps to Follow

❶ Review the major events of the story with students. List the events on the chalkboard in correct sequence. Explain to students that they will be drawing pictures of the events listed at right to retell the story.

First the fox fell into the well.

Then the fox tricked the goat into jumping down the well.

Next the fox climbed onto the goat to get out of the well.

Finally the fox left the goat in the well.

❷ Have students color and cut out the well pattern. Have them cut two slits as marked. (Younger students might need help cutting the slits.)

❸ Show students how to insert the construction paper strip into the slits of the well. Demonstrate how to move the strip until a blank section fills the opening. This is where they will draw the picture. Have them continue to move the strip and draw until they have completed the story.

❹ Divide the class into pairs, and have students share their pull-through pictures as they retell the fable.

The Fox and the Goat

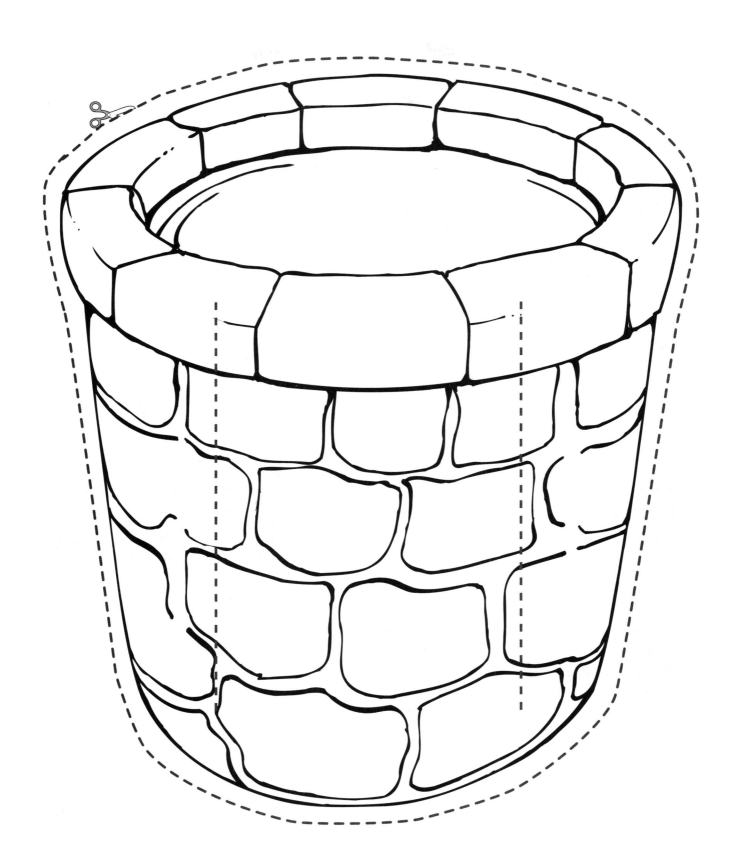

69

Look Before You Leap

Materials

- page 71, two copies reproduced for each student
- scissors
- 3½" x 6" (9 x 15 cm) pieces of construction paper, two for each student
- 2½" x 5" (6.5 x 13 cm) piece of light-colored construction paper, one for each student
- crayons, colored pencils, marking pens
- hole punch
- 18" (45.5 cm) pieces of yarn
- glue

Steps to Follow

❶ Ask students to recall the meaning of the moral "Look before you leap." Work together to brainstorm a list of situations that require "looking before you leap."

> before crossing a busy street
> before diving into a pool or lake
> before skating across a frozen lake
> before trying to pet a dog you don't know
> before opening the door for someone you don't know

❷ Guide students through the following steps to make a minibook about the moral:

a. Cut out each book form. Fold over the flap as marked.

b. On the top of the flap, write an example of when you should "look before you leap."

c. Lift the flap and draw a picture in the box to go with your example. Then refold the form.

d. Repeat the steps with all four forms.

e. Write the book title on the smaller piece of construction paper as a label for the front cover. Glue it to the cover. Use the other piece of construction paper for the back cover.

f. Punch three holes along the left-hand side of the cover pieces and the book pages. Use a piece of yarn to lace the book together.

The Fox and the Goat

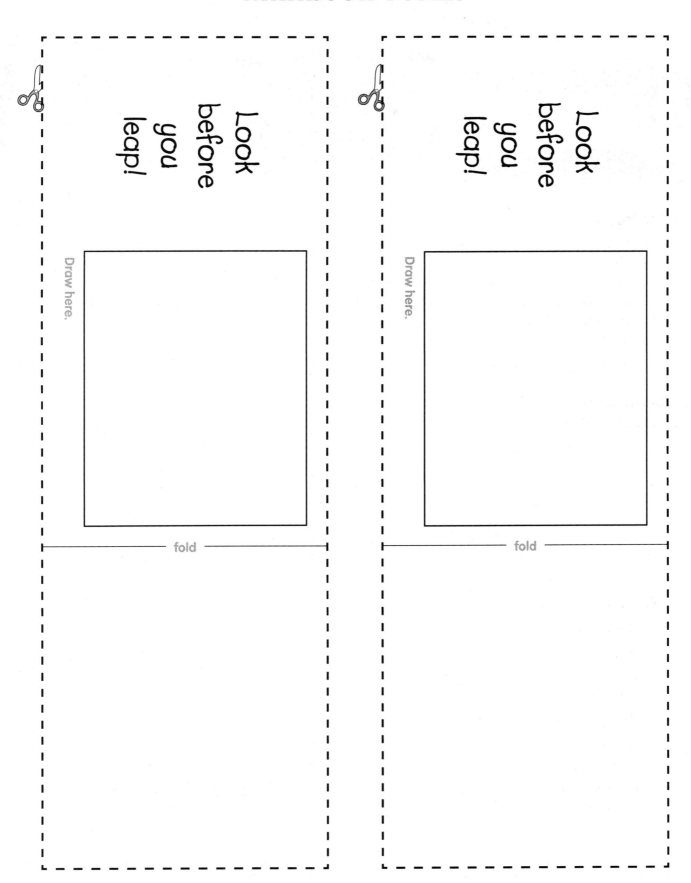

Look
before
you
leap!

Draw here.

fold

Look
before
you
leap!

Draw here.

fold

Literature Pockets—Aesop's Fables • EMC 2733

Name: _____

Alike and Different

The animals in the story are like real animals in some ways:

1. _____

2. _____

3. _____

The animals in the story are different from real animals in these ways:

1. _____

2. _____

3. _____

Draw the animals from the fable.

Mrs. Fox	**Mr. Goat**

The Fox and the Goat

The Fox and the Stork

Pocket Label and Bookmark .... **page 74**
Have students use these reproducibles to make
The Fox and the Stork pocket label and bookmark.
(See page 2.)

**The Story of
The Fox and the Stork** .... **pages 75–77**
Share and discuss this fable about a fox who
learns that it isn't nice to play tricks on your friends.
Reproduce the story on pages 76 and 77 for students.
Use the teaching ideas on page 75 to preview, read,
and review the story. Follow up with the "More to
Explore" activities.

What Is the Moral? .... **page 78**
Use this reproducible to review the meaning of the
fable's moral with students. Have students rewrite the
moral in their own words and then apply it to real-life
situations.

**The Fox and
the Stork Puppets** .... **pages 79 and 80**
Students will love using these three-dimensional stick
puppets of the fox and the stork to retell the fable.

Write a Play .... **pages 81–83**
Students write original dialog for the fox and the stork
to use with their stick puppets. They perform the play
for classmates or other students at school.

A Courtesy Chain .... **pages 84 and 85**
Students explore the importance of treating others
the way they want to be treated. They create a paper
chain of children showing the moral written on the
front and examples of the moral written on the back.

The Fox and the Stork

Story characters:

Fox

Stork

Moral of the story:

Treat others the way you want to be treated.

I liked this story:

☐ Yes

☐ No

This bookmark belongs to

_____

(your name)

The Fox and the Stork

Share The Fox and the Stork

Preview the Story

State the title of the fable, and have students read aloud the names of the characters listed on the bookmark. Distribute copies of the fable (pages 76 and 77), and have students preview the pictures. Invite students who are unfamiliar with the fable to predict what happens between the fox and the stork.

Read the Story

Read the fable aloud as students follow along. Encourage students to track the text and underline or frame key words. List and discuss any unfamiliar words, such as *delicious*, *shallow*, *lap*, *complain*, *snout*, *rumbling*, and *blame*. Point out picture clues and context clues that help explain parts of the fable. After you have read the fable aloud, encourage students to reread it independently or with a partner.

Review the Story

Ask questions such as the following to help students recall important details about the characters, setting, and plot of the fable:

- What joke did the fox play on the stork?
- How do you think the stork felt when she couldn't eat any of the soup?
- Why did the stork invite the fox to dinner after what he had done?
- Why couldn't the fox eat any of the stew the stork had made?
- What lesson did the stork teach the fox?

More to Explore

- The Prefix *Un*

  Remind students that the fox had been unkind to the stork. Ask, "What does *unkind* mean?" Explain that the *un* part of the word means "not." Write the following words on the chalkboard: *unkind, unfair, unhappy, unable*. Read each word aloud and ask students to explain what the word means. Then have students use each of the words in oral or written sentences.

- Friends

  The fox was unkind to the stork. Ask students to consider whether the two could ever be friends again, and how this could be accomplished. Have students share their ideas with the class. Extend the lesson by having students pretend to be the fox and write a letter of apology to the stork.

- Figurative Language

  Explain to students that some expressions have special meanings that are not the same as the meanings of the individual words. Point out the expressions "her face fell" and "his mouth began to water" in the fable. Have students explain the actual meanings of those expressions. Extend the lesson by having students draw pictures of the literal and actual meanings.

The Fox and
the Stork

The Fox and the Stork

Early one evening, Fox invited Stork over for dinner. When Stork arrived, she smelled something delicious cooking. "I wonder what Fox has made for dinner?" she thought. "It smells so good my mouth is watering."

When Stork sat down at the table, her face fell. Fox had served the delicious soup in a shallow bowl! Fox could lap up the soup, but Stork could get only a few drops with her long, narrow beak.

"I'm sorry that you don't like the soup," said Fox as he laughed behind Stork's back.

Stork did not complain about dinner. She did not say anything about the way Fox treated her. She just said, "Will you come to my house for dinner tomorrow night?"

Fox quickly said, "Yes," because he knew that Stork was a good cook.

The next evening, Fox hurried over to Stork's house. When he arrived, his mouth began to water at the delicious smell. "I wonder what tasty meal Stork has cooked for me?"

Fox hurried to sit down at the dinner table. Stork had made a delicious stew full of tiny bits of meat and vegetables. Fox could hardly wait to taste the stew.

Stork brought the stew to the table in a tall jar with a narrow mouth. Now it was Stork's turn to laugh. She stuck her long, narrow beak into the jar and ate the delicious stew.

Poor Fox sat by and watched. He tried to get his snout into the jar to reach the stew. He could only lick off the bits that were left on the mouth of the jar.

After dinner, Fox headed home, his stomach rumbling with hunger. He knew he could not blame his friend. He had been unkind to Stork. He learned that you must treat others the way you want to be treated.

Name: _____

What Is the Moral?

A fable is a short story that teaches a lesson.
That lesson is called a moral.

Find the moral of "The Fox and the Stork." Write it here.

_____

_____

Explain what the moral means.

_____

_____

Give a real-life example of the moral. Tell about your own experience or about someone you know.

_____

_____

_____

_____

_____

_____

_____

_____

The Fox and the Stork

The Fox and the Stork Puppets

Materials

- page 80, reproduced for each student
- crayons, colored pencils, marking pens
- scissors
- glue
- craft sticks
- legal-sized envelopes

Steps to Follow

❶ Guide students through the following steps to make stick puppets of the fox and the stork:

    a. Color and cut out all the puppet pieces.

    b. Fold the fox's snout and the stork's beak as marked. Glue each piece onto the animal's face.

    c. Glue each face onto a craft stick.

    d. Fold the paper jar as marked to stand it up.

❷ Have students use their puppets to retell the fable to a partner. Have the storyteller sit behind a table, hold the fox and stork above the table, and put the bowl and jar on the table as needed.

❸ When students finish retelling the fable, have them store the puppets in an envelope inside the pocket.

Puppet Patterns

jar

fold

bowl

paste   paste
fold   fold

paste   paste
fold   fold

Literature Pockets—Aesop's Fables • EMC 2733

Write a Play

Materials
- pages 82 and 83, reproduced for each student
- overhead transparencies of pages 82 and 83
- overhead projector and markers
- stick puppets from the previous activity (pages 79 and 80)
- butcher paper and marking pens (optional)

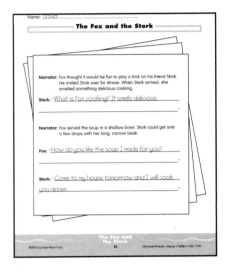

Steps to Follow

❶ Reread the fable to students. Stop at each dialog and have students read aloud the spoken words.

❷ Display the first transparency. Explain to students that they will be writing a play about the fox and the stork. Have them identify the three speaking roles (the fox, the stork, and the narrator). Explain the purpose of a narrator. Then read the narrator's lines with students. Read both the first and second transparency.

❸ Have students complete the fox and stork dialog in one of these ways:

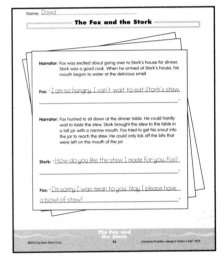

- As a class—Together decide what the animals will say. Write the sentences on the overhead transparency. Have students copy the sentences onto their forms.
- In small groups—Have group members read the narrator's lines and then decide what the animals will say. Have members write the sentences on their own forms.
- Individually—Have more advanced students complete the script on their own.

❹ Have pairs of students use their puppets to perform the play for a group of classmates or for another group of students at school.

❺ Extend the activity by having students use butcher paper and marking pens to make a backdrop for their play.

The Fox and the Stork

Name: _____

The Fox and the Stork

Narrator: Fox thought it would be fun to play a trick on his friend Stork. He invited Stork over for dinner. When Stork arrived, she smelled something delicious cooking.

Stork: "_____

_____ "

Narrator: Fox served the soup in a shallow bowl. Stork could get only a few drops with her long, narrow beak.

Fox: "_____

_____ "

Stork: "_____

_____ "

Name: _____

The Fox and the Stork

Narrator: Fox was excited about going over to Stork's house for dinner. Stork was a good cook. When he arrived at Stork's house, his mouth began to water at the delicious smell.

Fox: "_____

_____"

Narrator: Fox hurried to sit down at the dinner table. He could hardly wait to taste the stew. Stork brought the stew to the table in a tall jar with a narrow mouth. Fox tried to get his snout into the jar to reach the stew. He could only lick off the bits that were left on the mouth of the jar.

Stork: "_____

_____"

Fox: "_____

_____"

Literature Pockets—Aesop's Fables • EMC 2733

A Courtesy Chain

Materials

- page 85, reproduced for students
- 6" x 18" (15 x 45.5 cm) construction paper
- scissors
- crayons, colored pencils, marking pens

Steps to Follow

Guide students through the following steps to make a chain of paper dolls:

❶ Fold the construction paper into fourths and refold it accordion style as shown.

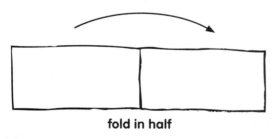

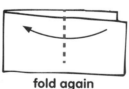

fold in half

fold again

open and fold accordion style

❷ Cut out the paper doll pattern. Lay it on the construction paper so that the arms and feet touch the folded edges on both sides.

❸ Trace around the pattern and then carefully cut out the paper doll. Do not cut across the folded edges of the hands and feet. Leave them attached. Unfold the construction paper to show a chain of four connected paper dolls.

❹ Write the moral on the children as shown. Leave space below the writing.

❺ Color the children in the chain, alternating boys and girls. Cut out a triangle between the legs of the boy dolls. Color the boys to show them wearing pants and a shirt. Color the girls to show them wearing a dress.

❻ On the back of each child, write one way you want to be treated.

The Fox and the Stork

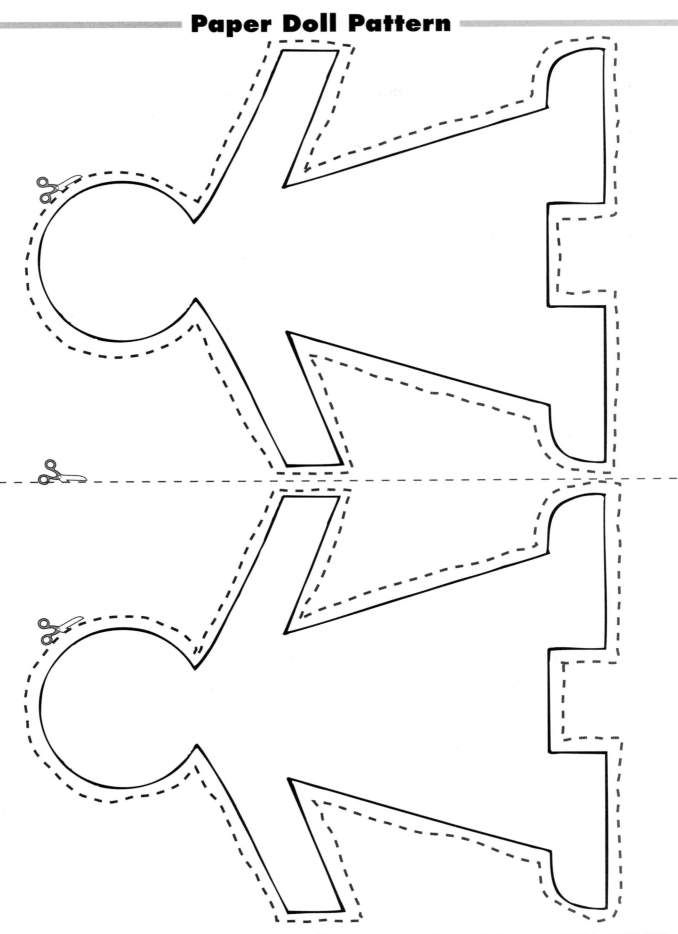

Literature Pockets—Aesop's Fables • EMC 2733

The Cat, the Rooster, and the Mouse

Have students use these reproducibles to make The Cat, the Rooster, and the Mouse pocket label and bookmark. (See page 2.)

Share and discuss this fable about a little mouse who learns not to judge others by their looks. Reproduce the story on pages 89 and 90 for students. Use the teaching ideas on page 88 to preview, read, and review the story. Follow up with the "More to Explore" activities.

Use this reproducible to review the meaning of the fable's moral with students. Have students rewrite the moral in their own words and then apply it to real-life situations.

Students refer to the fable as they complete a chart describing the cat and the rooster. Then they write their own description of the little mouse.

With an ink pad, fine-tipped marking pens, and the tips of their fingers, students create charming pictures of the cat, the rooster, and the little mouse. Then they fill in thought bubbles for each animal.

After reading and discussing the various fables in this book, students write their own original fable. This activity may be done as a class, in small groups, or by individuals working independently.

The Cat, the Rooster, and the Mouse

Story characters:

Young Mouse

Mother Mouse

Cat

Rooster

Moral of the story:

Judge others by their actions, not by their looks.

I liked this story:

☐ Yes

☐ No

This bookmark belongs to

_____

(your name)

Share The Cat, the Rooster, and the Mouse

Preview the Story

State the title of the fable, and have students read aloud the names of the characters listed on the bookmark. Distribute copies of the fable (pages 89 and 90), and have students preview the pictures. Invite students who are unfamiliar with the fable to predict how a young mouse reacts to seeing a cat and a rooster for the first time.

Read the Story

Read the fable aloud as students follow along. Encourage students to track the text and underline or frame key words. List and discuss any unfamiliar words, such as *begging*, *fear*, *strange*, *creatures*, *hummed*, *flapping*, *horrible*, *rooster*, *harmed*, *escape*, and *snuggled*. Point out picture clues and context clues that help explain parts of the fable. After you have read the fable aloud, encourage students to reread it independently or with a partner.

Review the Story

Ask questions such as the following to help students recall important details about the characters, setting, and plot of the fable:

- What did the little mouse want to do?
- Why did the little mouse return home so soon?
- How did the little mouse describe the cat?
- How did the little mouse describe the rooster?
- Which animal frightened the little mouse more, the cat or the rooster? Why?
- Which of the two animals was more dangerous to the little mouse?
- What lesson did the little mouse learn?

More to Explore

- Verbs and Adjectives

  Review the definitions of a verb and adjective with the class. Then have students fold a sheet of paper in half and label one half "verbs" or "action words" and the other half "adjectives" or "describing words." Ask students to find six examples of each kind of word in the story and list the words in the correct half of the paper.

- What Do Chickens Eat?

  Provide books about chickens. Explain to students that while the story says that roosters (male chickens) eat seeds, that is not the only thing they eat. Have students work in small groups to find other things that chickens eat. When each group has completed a list, share the results with the class. Have them decide if a mouse would or would not be safe from a rooster.

The Cat, the Rooster, and the Mouse

The Cat, the Rooster, and the Mouse

A young mouse had been begging his mother to let him leave their mouse hole. He wanted to see more of the world. At last the day came when his mother agreed to let him go outside. "Don't stay out too late," she told her son. "Come back soon and tell me about everything you see."

The little mouse was only gone a few minutes. He was shaking with fear when he returned. "Oh, Mother!" he cried. "I saw two strange creatures in the outside world."

"What did the creatures look like?" asked his mother.

"The first one was pretty," said the little mouse. "It was covered in soft gray fur and had big green eyes. It waved its long furry tail at me. All the time it hummed a pretty song. It looked like a nice creature."

"What was the other creature like?" asked his mother.

"The other creature looked like a terrible monster. It was covered with feathers. It had red skin on top of its head and another piece hanging down in front. It had long nails on its toes. The monster walked up to me, scratching the dirt with its nails and flapping its arms against its sides. Then the monster opened its pointed mouth and screamed 'Cock-a-doodle-doo!' right in my face. I ran home as fast as I could."

"My son," said his mother, "that horrible monster was just a rooster. It wouldn't have hurt you. It eats seeds. The other creature was a cat. It may have looked nice, but it would have harmed you. Cats like to eat mice. You were lucky to escape with your life."

The little mouse snuggled closer to his mother. She gave him a big hug. "Just remember to be more careful the next time you go outside. Judge others by their actions, not by their looks."

The Cat, the Rooster, and the Mouse

Name: _____

What Is the Moral?

A fable is a short story that teaches a lesson.
That lesson is called a moral.

Find the moral of "The Cat, the Rooster, and the Mouse." Write it here.

_____

_____

Explain what the moral means.

_____

_____

Give a real-life example of the moral. Tell about your own experience or about someone you know.

_____

_____

_____

_____

_____

_____

_____

_____

**The Cat, the Rooster,
and the Mouse**

What the Mouse Saw

Little Mouse

The chubby little mouse was covered in soft black fur. His tiny eyes were as shiny as black beans. His long tail was always moving around.

The chubby little mouse was curious about the world outside his home. He wanted to see other places and other animals. He thought he was brave enough to go off by himself.

The curious little mouse found out was not brave. He was scared of the loud noises and strange animals he met. He wanted to be home with his mother where he felt safe.

Materials

- writing paper
- glue
- 9" x 12" (23 x 30.5 cm) construction paper
- crayons, colored pencils, marking pens

Steps to Follow

❶ Draw a two-column chart on the chalkboard as shown, leaving room for a third column later.

	cat	rooster
appearance		
actions		

❷ Reread to students the description of the cat from the fable. Have students listen for words and phrases to complete the cat section of the chart. List those characteristics on the chart.

❸ Repeat Step 2 for the description of the rooster.

❹ Add a third column to the chart and label it "mouse." Ask students to pretend to be an animal that had never seen the little mouse. Have them brainstorm a list of phrases that describe a mouse's appearance and actions. Record their responses.

❺ After completing the chart, ask students to write about the little mouse. Tell them to include the information from the chart. You may choose to work with students to complete the description or have them work independently. Students may complete the project on the computer.

	cat	rooster	mouse
appearance	soft gray fur, big green eyes, long furry tail	feathers, red skin on top of head and hanging down, long toenails, pointed mouth	white fur, long pink tail, pink nose and eyes
actions	smiled, waved, hummed	scratched dirt, flapped arms, screamed	looked and listened, ran home, talked to mother, shook with fear

❻ Have students glue their description onto construction paper and draw the little mouse somewhere on the page. Invite students to read aloud their descriptions.

The Cat, the Rooster, and the Mouse

Fingerprint Characters

Materials

- black ink pads
- pencils with new erasers
- scrap paper
- 4" x 7" (10 x 18 cm) white construction paper
- 6" x 9" (15 x 23 cm) black construction paper
- glue
- scissors
- moist towels (for wiping hands)
- fine-tipped marking pens

Steps to Follow

❶ Demonstrate how to use an ink pad, a pencil eraser, and your fingertips to make the following animals. Show how to use marking pens to draw the details on each face and body.

❷ Have students work in small groups, sharing an ink pad and a set of marking pens. Guide them through the following steps:

a. Practice making fingerprints using your little finger and thumb of one hand.

b. Make the mouse, cat, and rooster in a row at the bottom of the white paper. Leave plenty of space between the animals.

c. Draw a thought bubble above each animal. Inside the bubble, write what the animal might have thought when he saw one or both of the other animals.

d. Glue the white paper to the black paper. Draw a border around the white paper to frame your picture.

My Own Fable

Materials
- writing paper
- construction paper slightly larger than the writing paper
- stapler
- crayons, colored pencils, marking pens

Steps to Follow

❶ Use the fable of "The Lion and the Mouse" or "The Fox and the Stork" to model how to complete a story map. Draw a story map on the chalkboard, as shown at right. Reread the fable to students. Ask them to recall details to fill in the map.

❷ Work with students to write an original fable, or have partners or individuals work independently. Have students follow these steps:

a. Draw a story map like the one on the board.

b. Select one of the morals from the fables you have already read. Write this in the moral box. You will use this moral for your own original fable.

c. List the characters that will be in your fable.

d. List the problem that the main character will have to solve.

e. Plan how the problem will be solved. Tell what will happen at the beginning, middle, and end of the fable. Do not write complete paragraphs. Just list ideas.

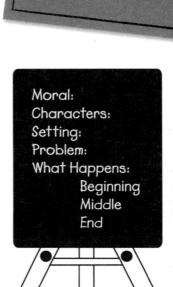

f. Use your story map to help you write your fable. Tell what happens to the characters. Describe how the characters look and what they do. Remember that your fable should teach a lesson—the moral of the story.

g. When you finish your fable, staple it between two sheets of construction paper to make the cover. Write a title and draw a picture on the front cover.

❸ Provide time for students to share their fables with classmates.

The Cat, the Rooster, and the Mouse

Note: Reproduce this evaluation sheet for students to complete after they have finished their Aesop's Fables book.

Name: _____

Aesop's Fables Evaluation

A fable is a short story that has a moral.
What is a moral?

_____

_____

Give an example of a moral.

_____

_____

Look back at the fables that you read. Find three new words that you learned.
Write your own sentences using those words.

_____

_____

_____

Look back at the activities that you did for the fables.
Which activity did you like the best? Why?

_____

_____

_____

Which activity did you like the least? Why?

_____

_____

_____

Name: _____

Aesop's Fables Evaluation

My favorite fable is _____.

I like it best because of these three reasons:

1. _____

   _____

2. _____

   _____

3. _____

This is my favorite character.

Draw here.

Character's name: _____

These words describe my favorite character.

_____

_____